THE ADVENTURES OF AVA AND RORY

AS TOLD BY AVA

By Jennifer Duncan Garrett

Illustrated By Sophie Van Dyne

Copyright © 2022 by Jennifer Duncan Garrett

All rights reserved. No portion of this book may be reproduced in any form or by any electronic or mechanical means, including information storage and retrieval systems - except in the case of brief quotations in articles or reviews - without permission in writing from its publisher, Jennifer Duncan Garrett. Copyright protection extends to all excerpts and previews by this author included in this book.

This novel is a work of fiction. Names, characters, businesses, places, events and incidents are either the products of the author's imagination or used in a fictitious manner.

All brand names and product names used in the book are trademarks, registered trademarks, or trade names of their respective holders. The author or publisher is not associated with any product or vendor in this book.

Illustration by Sophie Van Dyne

Ebook: 979-8-9871317-1-8
Paperback: 979-8-9871317-0-1
Hardback:979-8-9871317-2-5

"Hug your kids and hug them often
as tomorrow is not promised."

Jennifer Duncan Garrett

Dedicated to my beautiful daughter,
the late LTJG Morgan Lynn Garrett.
She was the Mom of these two little characters.

Our Mom adopted us from the local Humane Society in Pensacola, Florida. We were both a little scared at first, but that didn't last long. She showered us with hugs and kisses and we soon felt right at home.

Our Mom is the best! We sure do love her!

Mom goes to this place she refers to as "Work" almost everyday. We miss her when she is gone. We do a lot of sleeping but there are times we get a little restless. Especially Rory!

Rory can open anything.

Mom keeps our food in a large glass container.

He kept removing the lid and would jump in and eat.

Mom started hiding our food in the cabinet, but that didn't stop Rory. He could open the cabinet door and get right in. Mom finally had to put a 10 pound weight on the top to keep him out.

Mom always calls him a "Little Stinker". I don't know what that means, but it doesn't sound good.

I, on the other hand, am her "Little Princess".

One day as Mom left for work, when she shut the front door, for some reason it caused the back door to crack open. Rory of course had to go see what was going on.

He pushed the door open and stepped outside. I was all ready to take my morning nap, but found myself curious as well and stepped outside.

About that time a gust of wind blew the door shut. Rory was very good at opening things, but this one he could not.

He tried and tried, we both did but we could not open the door. It was very bright outside and very hot. I really wanted to take my nap, curled up on Mom's soft bed, but I couldn't.

Rory on the other hand was ready to explore. I being his sister, felt I should go along with him to try to keep him out of trouble. We heard loud noises coming from behind our apartment building. We saw a lot of people, so we thought we would go see what was going on.

As we got closer, we saw this large bowl of water. Rory stated he was thirsty and wanted to get a drink. When he got to the water, it was hard for him to reach. He climbed down the side a little, lost his balance and went splashing into the water.

He had never been in water before and didn't know what to do. I was scared as I didn't know how to help him and the people here at the large bowl of water were at the other end and didn't seem to see us.

Rory was splashing and wailing, just trying to keep his head above water.

About the time I thought he was going to go under for the last time, a little black and white dog came swimming by and said to Rory, "Hey, don't panic, just do what I'm doing. It's called the dog paddle."

Rory calmed down and started following the little black and white dog doing exactly what he was doing. They swam over to the steps and both got out.

By this time, the people saw they had been in the water and shooed them away. They ran toward me and Rory meowed, "Sis, come on, we've got to get out of here!"

All three of us made it under the fence. The little black and white dog asked Rory if he was ok. Once Rory caught his breath, he said, "yeah, I'm ok, thank you so much, you saved me.

By the way my name is Rory and this is my sister, Ava." The little black and white dog told us his name was Duncan and said he would like to be our friend.

About the time we said yes we would love to be friends, Duncan's Mom picked him up and carried him to their home. Duncan barked, "see you soon". We watched as he nuzzled his Mom's neck.

I was so ready for my nap and I was hungry. About that time I smelled this wonderful aroma coming from a moving object. People were referring to it as a Food Truck.

We watched as people lined up at the Food Truck. They would order and a man inside the truck would hand them the most incredible looking food I had ever seen. Rory and I were thinking the exact same thing at the exact same time. We had to get inside that Food Truck.

We waited what seemed to be hours for our chance to get inside. Once the last person in line had been given their order, the man inside stepped out to pick up some napkins that had flown away while he was serving food.

That was our chance and we took it! We were able to sneak behind him without him seeing us and jump in the Food Truck.

To our surprise, he just shut the door. He didn't come in. We were in there all alone with all of that deliciously smelling food. As I told you before, Rory could pretty much open anything. The containers the food was stored in was no challenge at all for Rory. He ripped them right off and we dug right in.

We ate...
and ate...
and ate!

At no time while we were stuffing ourselves did we realize the Food Truck was moving. It wasn't until the truck stopped abruptly that we realized it had been moving. We heard the man talking to someone.

He said he was in a hurry to get home as Hurricane Sally was making her way toward Pensacola Beach and he wanted to get back across the Pensacola Bay Bridge as soon as possible. He opened the door and put in boxes of supplies.

We decided we needed to get out of there before he saw the mess we had left him, so we scurried out before he got back with more boxes.

Once outside, everything was different. We no longer saw our apartment building. There was a lot of soft, white stuff that looked and felt a lot like our kitty box and a huge bowl of water, much, much bigger than the one behind our apartment building.

We were scared.

We had no place to go and we sure did miss our Mom.
About that time, the winds picked up and the large bowl of water had these waves that came crashing down on the white stuff. The sky got real dark and it also started raining.

The wind blew harder and we were getting soaked. We found shelter in a small hut right on the beach. We cuddled up together, both of us so scared. As the wind blew hard and loud against the small hut, it started taking on water.

Then out of no where the roof was gone. It had been torn away by the strong winds. We dug our claws deep into the wooden floor and held on for dear life. We wondered if we would ever make it home again.

We really missed our Mom.

Through the darkness we could see the floor of the hut was now a raft surrounded by water. The whirling wind was taking us further out to sea. I was so tired, I could barely hang on. Rory meowed loudly over the noise...

"if we by chance get thrown into the water, remember to dog paddle like Duncan taught us."

The winds and waves tore away our raft. We were both hanging on by a mere thread to the last piece of wood from the hut floor. We started dog paddling as the last piece of wood was taken from us.

We tried our best to stay together and keep our heads above water. The wind and the waves were so strong, they were taking the life right out of us. All I could think about was being at home, cuddled up with our Mom.

It was a United States Coast Guard helicopter. There appeared to be a person in a basket coming down straight at us. As the basket approached, the person inside picked us up and held us tight to their chest. We were then hoisted up to the helicopter!

Once inside and the doors closed, I heard a familiar voice. It sounded like Mom's good friend Mack. We looked and it was Mack! Oh WOW, we were so excited to see her!

Then, we heard another familiar voice say,

"YOU LITTLE STINKERS, HOW DID YOU GET ALL THE WAY OUT HERE?"

That beautiful voice was our Mom's. She was the co-pilot! When we heard her voice, we both jumped into her lap! We were so happy to see her and be safe in her arms.

Later that night when we were back at home, neither Rory or I would let Mom out of our sight. It had been a very long day. We were all very tired. We went to bed, snuggled up with Mom, me in her arms and Rory on top of her head. As we drifted into dream land, Mom kissed us both on the head and said, "I love you, my precious babies."

Safe in her arms, we went to sleep!

The Morgan Lynn Garrett Heart of Courage Foundation

Established
August 23, 2023

Morgan Lynn Garrett

10.22.1996 - 10.23.2020

Lieutenant Junior Grade (LTJG) Morgan Lynn Garrett of Pensacola, Florida, formerly of Weddington, North Carolina died October 23, 2020, during a training mission when the T-6B aircraft she and her instructor, Lieutenant Rhiannon Ross, were flying crashed into a residential area near Foley, Alabama. She had just celebrated her 24th birthday the day before. Morgan was born October 22, 1996, in Charlotte, North Carolina. She was a spunky, happy child with a big heart and big smile that never outgrew her. She was a devoted daughter, friend, granddaughter, niece, and cousin. From an early age, she wanted to serve her country in some capacity. After a very successful running career at Weddington High School (Two Time All-State Girls Team in Cross Country, and 2015 Winter North Carolina State Champion 4×400 Relay Team to name a few), she received her appointment to the United States Coast Guard Academy in New London, Connecticut. While at the academy, she majored in Marine and Environmental Sciences, ran middle distance for her track team, and served as the Regimental Activities Officer her First Class year. She graduated from the Coast Guard Academy in May 2019.

Charities

Morgan was passionate about serving her community. Her courageousness, uplifting spirit, and big heart carries on through the foundation to support the following charities.

The Morgan Lynn Garrett
Heart Of Courage Scholarship

This Scholarship is given in memory and honor of Morgan Lynn Garrett, an Alumni of Weddington High School. Morgan was a charismatic athlete and proved to be a courageous leader both on and off the field. After high school, Morgan made the brave and honorable decision to serve our country by accepting an appointment to the United States Coast Guard Academy. After four years at the Academy, Morgan graduated as an officer of the United States Coast Guard with her first assignment being Navy Flight School, Pensacola Florida. As an airman in the Coast Guard, Morgan continued to grow as a person and displayed even greater degrees of leadership and courage. In October 2020 Morgan tragically lost her life in a plane crash, but her legacy will live on for years to come. This scholarship was created to honor two students of courage and good character that display the traits Morgan is most remembered for.

American Humane

Morgan's love for animals not only helped inspire this book, but also the Foundation's desire to help shelter animals find good homes. Both Ava and Rory were shelter animals. They were two very lucky kitties to have had such a great Mom! The American Humane's Pups4Patriots™ program trains dogs in need of forever homes to become service animals for veterans. Please check out their website for more information regarding this wonderful program.

Helping A Hero

From a very early age, Morgan wanted to serve her country in some capacity. In high school she received a letter from the United States Coast Guard Academy asking her to consider the Academy and the possibility of running for their cross country and track teams. From that moment on, she decided the United States Coast Guard was how she would serve her country. Now through the Foundation, we continue her desire to help those who have so bravely served and fought for our country.

Morgan taught me to make every day a good day. She taught me to be loud, to laugh, and to do whatever it takes to make other people smile. She taught me that no kind act goes unnoticed, and that even the little things can change someone's whole life. Morgan taught me to be fearless and to love others with all my heart. I hope to live every day just like Morgan did.

♥ Katie

The thing that Morgan taught me was a little morale goes a long way. She consistently was a ray of sunshine at CGA and brought joy to the winters of Connecticut.

♥   Deborah

FLY

HIGH

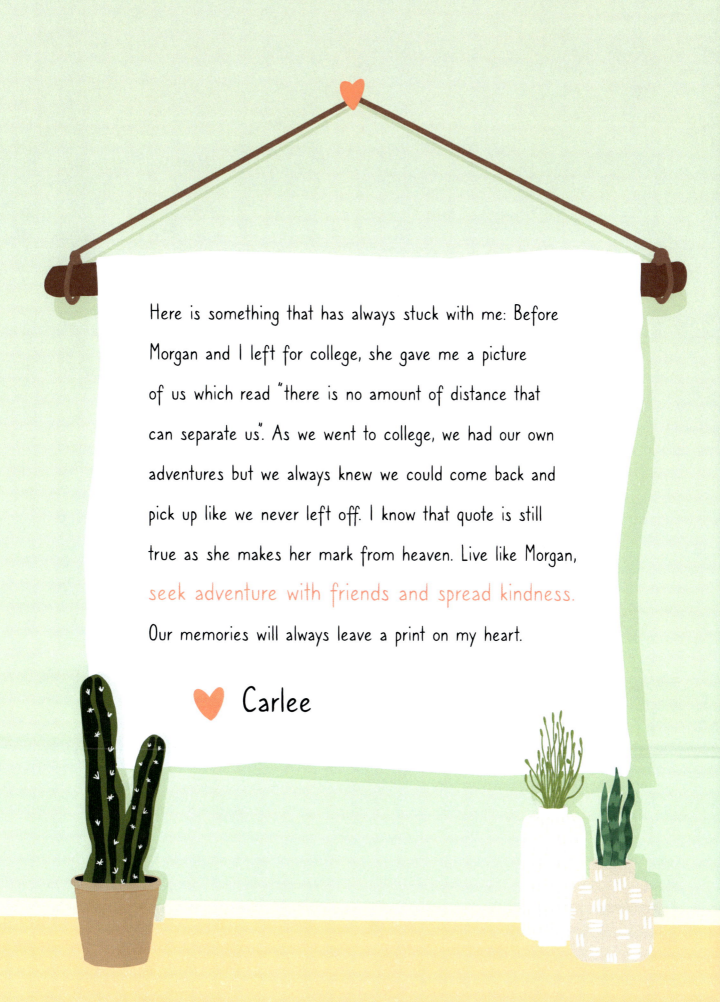

Here is something that has always stuck with me: Before Morgan and I left for college, she gave me a picture of us which read "there is no amount of distance that can separate us". As we went to college, we had our own adventures but we always knew we could come back and pick up like we never left off. I know that quote is still true as she makes her mark from heaven. Live like Morgan, seek adventure with friends and spread kindness. Our memories will always leave a print on my heart.

♥ Carlee

Two of the most amazing qualities about Morgan were her courage and confidence. She never shied away from a challenge. If others were reluctant or timid, she would be the one to take charge. Her ability to be a leader and seize opportunity were so important to her success, and in defining who she was. Often times when I feel overwhelmed or stressed, I think about Morgan and find strength in her spirit. Morgan was an inspiration to everyone to be bold, brave, and strong.

♥ James

ALWAYS bring your own SUNSHINE
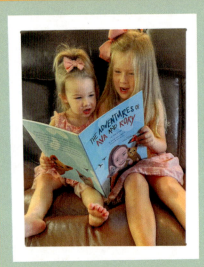

Morgan was like my sister and we bickered and fought like it. But I always knew that she had my back. Even through all of the fighting, I knew she was someone I could rely on, and when I needed it she was there, so I always tried to be the same for her and others. She absolutely taught me that *no matter what, loyalty in a friendship, or any relationship, goes a really long way.* Nothing is too big to sacrifice loyalty in a true friendship.

♥ Ryan

Oh my Morgs. Where to even begin. This girl taught me so much about life. You truly couldn't be in a bad mood around her. Morgan and I met in high school, so I had tears flowing often because when you're 16 everything is the end of the world. So she would allow me 5 minutes to cry, and then tell me to move on. Morgan would let me cry and then make me laugh until I cried again, all within the same 5 minutes. One of things she always told me was that we will never get this exact moment or day back, so why waste it upset? Something that always stood out to me was her little (tall) self being able to be so logical at such a young age. I have said it a million times and will say it again, to know her was to love her. And I haven't spent over 5 minutes upset since she has passed away, because I know she wouldn't want anymore time wasted.

♥ Mallory

At a pivotal point in my life, it was Morgan who encouraged me to pull myself together and pursue my dream of becoming an engineer. Morgan believed in me when I did not believe in myself, but I believed in her. Thankfully, I took her advice. Morgan's encouragement and empowering words inspired me and stuck with me for the years that followed. Since then, Morgan has continued to inspire me to challenge myself and those around me to break the barriers that would otherwise hold us back. Without that big push from Morgan, I would not be where I am today, or more importantly, be on the road to where I am headed. I believe that Morgan helped change the trajectory of my life. And for that — I am forever grateful.

♥ Charles

The things I learned from Morgan are:

Don't hesitate to tell your friends "I love you!" Never be afraid to get a few scratches and scrapes. Your friends will be there for you with band-aids. Be your own strength... And be it for someone who needs it.

 Lacey

Morgan enjoyed making the most of every moment, and never let anyone rain on her parade. Once, she decided we were going to play tennis for fun one afternoon, (neither of us knew how to play) and the courts were closed... so what does Morgan do? She starts hitting the tennis ball as far as she can in the empty parking lot, admittedly making the game even more fun. She was never afraid or embarrassed about anything, only looking to make memories and get the most out of life. She taught me how to *truly live in the present moment and find joy in unexpected places.*

♥ Mack

BE HAPPY

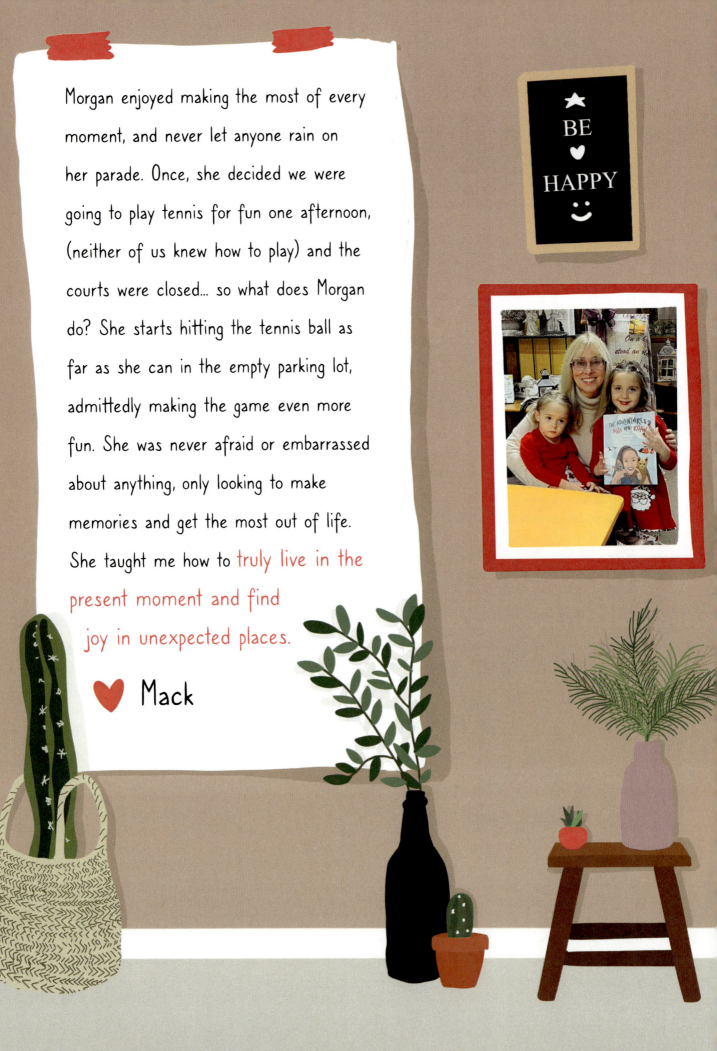

A note from the author

I would like to thank my family and friends for encouraging me to write this story. Seeing all the pictures, watching little videos Morgan had taken of her cats and remembering her laughter as she spoke so lovingly about them, were the seeds that sprouted into this little story about Ava and Rory. She so loved these two and the role of being their Mom!

Writing this book helped bring joy back into my life. Losing Morgan at such a young age when she was in the prime of her young life, living her dream, is the hardest thing through which I have ever had to live. Writing this book helped me navigate the grieving process. It helped me laugh again and find joy in the little things. For you parents reading this to your children, my hope is that you enjoy this time with them. Being a kid is such a "short season". Enjoy them while you can and please don't ever take these days for granted.

I would also like to thank Sophie Van Dyne for the beautiful illustrations. You brought this story to life with pictures. I am so thankful you said "yes" that Saturday morning over breakfast. Working with you on this project has been wonderful. I know Morgan would have loved this too!

Last, but definitely not least, I would like to thank the Men and Women of the United States Coast Guard as well as your families for your love and support. You are an amazing family and I want to thank you for letting me be a part of that family, but mostly thank you for loving and honoring "my girl"!

I have added some pictures of Morgan with Ava and Rory that helped inspire this book. I hope you enjoy them. Also, I have added a few of my favorites from the Coast Guard.

All proceeds from the sales of this book will be going to the Morgan Lynn Garrett Heart of Courage Foundation. Funds will be distributed to different charities we know Morgan would have loved as well as the scholarships given in Morgan's memory.

A note from the illustrator

I met Morgan on the very first day of seventh grade. From the beginning we shared a special bond. She felt like a sister. We spent so much time together for the next six years. We ran cross country and track, went to summer camps together, and had countless sleepovers. We talked about everything, we laughed a lot, and we cried sometimes, too. We had so much fun! When it came time for college, we went in very different directions. Morgan went to the U.S. Coast Guard Academy, while I headed to art school. It turned out that even with all of that time away from each other, our friendship continued to thrive. We got together whenever we could, and we were always able to pick up right where we had left off.

I have no words for what it felt like to lose Morgan. At first, I refused to believe she was gone. I missed her so much that it hurt. Even now, there isn't a day that goes by that I don't think to myself, "What would Morgan say? What would Morgan do?"

When Jennifer asked me to illustrate "The Adventures of Ava and Rory," I was so incredibly honored. I was also a bit afraid of how painful it would be, but even so, I knew that I wanted to do it. Meeting with Jennifer and connecting with some of Morgan's other close friends helped me feel closer to Morgan. All of this has led me to understand the value of real friendship. To kids of all ages who might be reading this book, I just want to remind you to truly cherish your friendships every day. A friend for life will always be with you, no matter what happens. And that is a very good thing. I am sure Morgan would agree.

Made in the USA
Columbia, SC
23 October 2024

9eabbded-1f3f-404c-a0d5-605643d09e9fR01